One More Year:
The Hilltop Pact

*A 10-Minute
Environmental Comedy-Drama*

AVIS KALFSBEEK

An adapted scene from
One More Year

Copyright & Licensing

One More Year: The Hilltop Pact

Licensing

Any *public* performance requires a free, simple performance license from the author.

Play Licensing: Any public performance requires a free, simple performance license from the

author.

To request permission, please submit a request to the Contact form at

www.AvisKalfsbeek.com.

Please credit all performances as:

One More Year: The Hilltop Pact by Avis Kalfsbeek

If you do perform it — anywhere, big or small — I'd love an invitation or a photo.

Thank you for keeping the *One More Year* pact alive.

Contents

About the Play

This 10-minute play is adapted from *One More Year*, the first book in the *Pedro the Water Dog Saves the Planet* series. In the book, Tilly is training for her first Ironman in the northwest mountain town of Sandglass, coached by her best friend Camas and supported by an unlikely team of quirky locals and Pedro, her loyal water dog.

At its core, *One More Year* is a joyful, irreverent eco-adventure about friendship, determination, and the simple idea that saving the planet starts with keeping our stuff just a little longer. Tilly's mantra—*One More Year, keep your stuff longer, people!*—is the spark that drives her mission to slow down overconsumption and inspire others to do the same.

This short play zooms in on one small but meaningful moment: a hilltop conversation where a hike becomes a pact. This adaptation keeps the heart of that scene while adding a theatrical twist: Pedro speaks directly to the audience, and an optional chorus offers visual symbolism. The piece maintains the same blend of humor, honesty, and affection found in the book.

It is intentionally simple to stage: a rock, a view, a heavily-stuffed backpack, and a story that speaks for itself. Perfect for classrooms, community groups, living rooms, outdoor gatherings, or any space where a small cast can bring a big-hearted idea to life.

If you enjoy this moment, you can read the full book (free eBook download available at aviskalfsbeek.com/book1free) and follow the whole adventure—one swim, one run, one ride, and one pact at a time.

Consider this play a tiny, theatrical echo of the book: a reminder to slow down, pay attention, and choose to keep your stuff... one more year.

How to Perform This Play

PERFORMANCE NOTES AND STAGING

This 10-Minute Play is intentionally simple. You can perform it with:

Cast Size

3 actors (**Tilly, Camas, Pedro**), or 3 actors plus an optional **Chorus** of Overconsumers and Keepers.

Space / Setting

Any small open area works: a patch of floor, a corner of a stage, a classroom, a spot under a tree. The "hilltop" is symbolic—one rock or natural-looking object (or simply an empty space the actors gesture toward) is enough to establish the setting.

Props (*Minimal and Flexible*)

One overstuffed backpack for Camas, which contains the following items (or similar), or you may **mime** pulling them out of the backpack.

The "Clutter" Items: Decorative cat statue, glittery ice skate (or boot), jar of pickles, rubber chicken, and a pizza slice.

One set of handlebars (real, cardboard, or improvised). *Note: The handlebars start in Camas's backpack and are later used by Pedro.*

One small cloth for Tilly.

Optional Chorus Items:

A bag or accessory for each **Overconsumer** (e.g., tote stuffed with visible "clutter").

One single meaningful object for each **Keeper**.

Everything else can be imagined.

Tone

Playful, warm, slightly chaotic (Camas), steady (Tilly), and aware (Pedro).

The humor should feel kind, not mocking.

The pact at the end should land softly, not theatrically heavy.

Running the Show

This play requires minimal production support:

No lighting, sound cues, or elaborate staging tricks are required.

Just actors, a story, and enough heart to carry it.

Note on Scripts

Please refer to the Licensing page for details on how to request permission and scripts.

Cast & Set

This short play, adapted from *One More Year*, features Tilly, Camas, Pedro, and an optional chorus of Overconsumers and Keepers. It runs about 10 minutes on stage and is set on a hillside trail overlooking a lake.

CAST

TILLY

Steady, idealistic, focused

CAMAS

Funny, impulsive, loyal

PEDRO

Dog narrator, in black with necktie of white curls, such as curled white ribbon; speaks directly to the audience

Optional Chorus:

THE OVERCONSUMERS

One or more performers who exaggerate clutter and distraction. They carry or wear obviously "too much"—an overstuffed bag, extra acces-

sories, or items that jingle or get in the way. Their energy should feel busy and humorous, never mocking.

THE KEEPERS

One or more performers who embody simplicity and care. Each holds a single meaningful object and moves with calm, intentional focus. Their presence provides contrast to the Overconsumers.

SET

A hillside trail. One large rock. An imagined lake below.

Optional: A side space for the Overconsumers (bags, bottles, clutter), and a side space for the Keepers (each with one meaningful object).

One More Year: The Hilltop Pact

A 10-Minute Environmental Comedy-Drama

One More Year: The Hilltop Pact (A 10-Minute Play)

(TILLY runs onstage, Pedro zig-zagging with joyful energy. She breathes deep, peaceful. A moment later—CAMAS stumbles in, panting, her backpack absurdly overstuffed. She wears a windbreaker, sunglasses, and slightly panicked joy.)

CAMAS

What the fungus, Tilly, slow down! Stop and smell the pine needles. I thought we were hiking, not chasing your personal best.

TILLY

I do smell them. As I sprint past them.

(CAMAS gives her a look—then melts, flopping down next to the boulder. Her pack hits the ground with a thud. She digs for something—maybe food—but the bag starts coughing up these items below, or similar items, pizza required.)

(Optional Chorus: Overconsumer(s) crowd in, mirroring her clutter. A Keeper(s) stands calm at the far side with one object.)

Items spill out quickly in rhythm; don't belabor each one. Items such as:

A phone charger

A crushed kombucha can

A worn journal

A hoodie

A half-knitted sock

A stress ball

An unopened lip balm

A mason jar labeled "Tea for Emergencies"

A tin of mints

A reusable straw

A second, tinier backpack

A cold slice of pizza

CAMAS

(frantically shoving things back in)

Hold on, hold on. Just need my hydration.

(She pulls out a small, ceramic, decorative cat statue, or similar.)

CAMAS

Ah. Not that. That's for good luck, and a conversation starter, obviously.

(She pulls out a single ice skate, or boot, covered in glitter.)

CAMAS

Oops. Wrong season. And wrong foot.

(She pulls out a jar of pickles and a rubber chicken.)

CAMAS

Right! Trail snacks. And backup emotional support. You never know when you need both a pickle and a good laugh.

(She reaches in deeper, struggling. Her arm disappears up to the elbow.)

CAMAS

(grunting)

Why is there always one more thing at the bottom...?

(She yanks out bicycle handlebars)

CAMAS

Oh....Yeah.

Those.

TILLY

(deadpan)

You brought handlebars?

CAMAS

(shrugs, totally casual)

For... ambiance.

(She tosses them down beside her or sets them leaning against the rock. They stay visible for Pedro later.)

(Camas is surrounded by clutter. TILLY quietly unfolds a small cloth, smooths it on the ground. She places one piece of fruit or bread in the center, ritual-like. A pause.)

(Then—PEDRO freezes, turns toward the audience, and raises a paw toward them.)

PEDRO

(steps toward Camas's pack, to audience)

I'll take those...

(He takes the handlebars. Holding them sideways, he begins "cycling" — legs, shoulders, whole body engaged.)

(PEDRO uses the handlebars throughout his monologue: holding them sideways like a pulpit, "cycling" with full-body pedaling motions to punch up facts, and adding exaggerated swerves when talking about being off-course. At key moments, he may turn the dowel vertically and use it like a microphone for comedic emphasis. Actor may interpret rhythm.)

(Optional Chorus: Overconsumers exaggerate their clutter; Keepers remain steady.)

PEDRO

(to audience)

Pedro Fact Check:

(pedals slowly, like weighing the number)

The average American owns over 300,000 items.

That's like... if every sock and spoon threw a family reunion.

The average hiker brings 293 of them on day trips.

(swerves handlebars toward CAMAS, holding the look until audience laughter lands)

Camas is shooting for the record.

(steady, pulpit grip, weight of fact)

We throw away 81 pounds of clothes every year.

That's a Great Dane... per person.

And none of us even get the dog.

We buy a million plastic bottles every minute.

That's faster than popcorn at the movies.

Only less tasty and way harder to recycle.

Every single day, 13 million phones get tossed. Most of them still work.

And we lease phones with plans to replace them before we even love them.

Imagine dating like that: "Hi, nice to meet you, oh sorry, my up-grade's here."

If stuff were snacks, we'd be buried in granola bars.

If stuff were dogs, we'd be the humans panicking in the shelter lobby.

If stuff were shoes, Camas would have…

(beat, drops handlebars low, conspiratorial)

…actually, never mind. She does have that many shoes.

(beat, gentle)

You can't climb the hill and carry the mall.

PEDRO

But maybe you don't have 300,000 items. Maybe you're doing great.

(He raises a paw, looking genuinely curious)

Let me ask you, has anyone here bought something new recently, maybe a jacket or a gadget, only to realize you already had something just like it tucked away in your closet or drawer?

(Pause for audience reaction, a knowing nod or two.)

It happens. That's why we're watching.

Let's watch.

(PEDRO rests the handlebars back on the crate, careful, like a ritual, then lies down.)

CAMAS

(Whispering to TILLY)

When did P start talking?

TILLY

(Shrugs)

(Back to the hilltop. CAMAS has narrowed it down to one bruised apple and the slice of pizza. TILLY has laid out a neat lunch—bread, cheese, fruit—on the cloth.)

CAMAS

What's that OMY on your shirt?

TILLY

(hesitates, then quietly)

It's a project I'm working on.

CAMAS

(takes a bite of pizza, with her mouth full)

I want to hear more.

TILLY

(laughs)

I see you brought one of your five food groups, cold pizza. What are the others again? Ice cream, huckleberries and?

CAMAS

Fries and naps.

TILLY

(shaking her head)

You're one of the strongest people I know despite what you put in your body.

CAMAS

(flexing a bicep)

Food rewards the watts. Why else would we suffer?

(She takes another bite.)

So what's the project?

TILLY

(looks out over the lake)

I see the coal cars passing over the lake on the tracks day after day and I feel so helpless.

CAMAS

What's the big deal? We need that coal to make the cities light up, right?

TILLY

(pulls her beanie down over her eyes to hide her tears, continues slowly)

Did you know that to get that coal they chop the mountain tops off and don't put them back?

CAMAS

(sits close, puts her arm around her)

Oh, you sensitive twit. I love your passion. I prefer passion for handsome guys, but thank goddess the earth has you.

TILLY

(beat—she pulls her beanie up, wipes her eyes, smiles)

OMY stands for One More Year. I had a dream about the Crying Indian.

(Camas looks confused.)

TILLY

You know, from the public service announcement in the 70s that tried to get people to stop littering and polluting. The roadsides were a dump of litter back then.

CAMAS

(teasing)

Indian is not PC.

TILLY

The dream told me we need a new kind of PSA to curb our over-consumption. That's One More Year.

CAMAS

(with her mouth full)

Huh?

TILLY

Keep your stuff longer. Don't just go get a new cell phone because you're eligible. Don't lease a new car because you can afford the payment. Don't buy that new outfit because you're depressed and bored.

CAMAS

(playfully nudges her stuffed backpack)

I did all of those things this month! What's wrong with that?

(TILLY doesn't laugh.)

CAMAS

You know I'm kidding, but I did think about doing those things.

TILLY

It's not just about clutter, Camas. The production of all that stuff generates 45% of all greenhouse gas emissions. If we buy less, the factories don't run as hard.

CAMAS

Wow. That's... a lot.

TILLY

It is. And consider this, the average piece of clothing is only worn seven times before it's thrown out. Seven. Think of the resources that went into that seven wears.

CAMAS

(nods slowly)

Seven wears. That makes my second, tinier backpack feel a little ridiculous.

TILLY

And one more: We're using natural resources 1.7 times faster than the Earth can regenerate them. We're running on an ecological deficit. Keeping what we have is the easiest way to slow that down.

TILLY

I know you can't change overnight.

CAMAS

Okay—wait.

Before I start "letting go," as you like to say…

I need to explain something.

These aren't just *things.*

They're… systems.

Tiny, portable, beautiful systems that keep my life from falling apart on any given Tuesday.

(points to objects as she goes)

This headlamp?

Necessary.

For power outages, night hikes, unexpected spiritual quests—

or when Pedro hides his ball under the deck and we all have to go spelunking to retrieve it.

PEDRO

(soft bark and head tilt)

Fact check: I do that… sometimes.

CAMAS

And this second headlamp?

Backup.

In case the first one fails or I need to lend one to a friend who insists they "don't need gear."

(looks at Tilly)

You know who you are.

This multitool?

It's not a multitool—it's a security blanket disguised as pliers.

These water bottles?

I know there are six.

But each one has a purpose.

Hot days, cold days, electrolyte days, panic days—PMS days--

and one of them still has a sticker from my first bike race.

I'm not getting rid of my race history.

That's emotional archaeology.

And this jacket?

Yes, it's torn.

Yes, the zipper is held together with a safety pin.

Yes, I have four others.

But this one...

This one has been with me through storms.

Literal storms.

And also... stormy storms.

Inside me.

I know it sounds ridiculous, but sometimes these beat-up things remind me I've survived stuff.

They're like little anchors I carry because part of me thinks if I drop them...

maybe I...

Maybe I won't know who I am without all my just-in-case gear.

So no, I'm not ready for a minimalist miracle on this hilltop.

I am a maximalist of memories.

A hoarder of hypotheticals.

A collector of "what ifs."

And honestly?

(raising her voice)

It's comforting.

It makes me feel prepared.

It makes me feel... safe.

(beat)

It makes me feel *me.*

TILLY

Okay — okay — wow.

That was... a lot of feelings for a hilltop.

Can we just take a beat?

Also, I kind of need to pee.

CAMAS

Now?! In the middle of my existential unraveling?!

TILLY

Yes. Now.

This is taking five for friendship.

CAMAS

(grumbling)

Fine. Take your tiny woodland moment.

I'll just... be here... reevaluating my entire identity.

(Tilly steps a few feet away, out of direct view but still in earshot. Pedro sits between them like a referee.)

CAMAS

(under her breath, scooping things back into the backpack with dramatic frustration)

I am not a minimalist. I am a survivalist with style.

Each of these things has a purpose — even if the purpose is unclear to you, thank you very much.

This jacket? Emotional armor.

This flashlight? Essential. For... vibes.

This second flashlight? Backup vibes.

This tiny backpack? A backup for my backup vibes.

(continuing to stuff things back in her pack dramatically, examines an item)

This isn't clutter — it's a support system.

A portable ecosystem of preparedness.

I'm not messy.

I'm layered.

Like a lasagna.

A very emotionally complex lasagna.

And yes, maybe I carry too many snacks —

but have I ever let *anyone* get hangry on my watch?

No. No, I have not.

You're welcome, planet.

Look, some people need crystals.

Some people need therapy.

I need... options.

(getting the last few things back into the pack—everything except the

handlebars—she pauses, then sighs)

PEDRO

(soft, sympathetic chuff)

Chuff

CAMAS

Don't you start.

You've got, like, one sock and a stick.

You don't understand my lifestyle.

(Tilly reenters, refreshed, brushing her hands.)

TILLY

Okay. I'm centered.

Are you done whisper-fighting with your backpack?

CAMAS

No.

TILLY

(gentle, but also seeing where this is going)

Okay, okay, calm down, sista.

You don't have to let go of anything today.

(beat — she shifts gears)

How about this:

Is there anything you're *about* to buy?

CAMAS

(thinks... then sheepishly)

I mean... I've been thinking I need a new mountain bike.

TILLY

A new mountain bike?

Really? Yours must be—what—two years old?

CAMAS

(offended in the way only best friends can offend each other)

Judged.

TILLY

(softens instantly)

Okay, okay. No judgment.

But... what if—hear me out—what if instead of a *whole new bike,*

you hit the bike swap and find one really cool used accessory...

and just keep your bike *one more year*?

CAMAS

(grumbling)

One more year, huh?

TILLY

Yeah.

And to commemorate your incredible emotional maturity,

you get your very own "One More Year" T-shirt.

(beat)

Which is technically a new thing...

but it's really just a thrift-store tee with custom iron-ons.

A *symbolic* new thing.

Planet-approved.

PEDRO

(one single bark of agreement, like stamping approval)

CAMAS

......Fine.

That... actually feels doable.

TILLY

(hugs Camas, looks her in the eyes)

If you wait one more year on one of those things, and your neighbor does too, and your mother, and her neighbor, it might slow down the zombie wastefulness.

(louder)

We need to slow all this down!

PEDRO

(two bright barks)

CAMAS

Sold. When do I get my shirt?

TILLY

(smiling)

I'll make you one tonight.

(A stillness. The lake seems to lean in to listen.)

CAMAS

(gentle now)

You're serious about OMY, aren't you?

TILLY

I am.

CAMAS

Then I am too.

(looks around)

Gotta pee too now.

(They rise. Tilly waits as Camas squats behind the large rock.)

CAMAS

(from behind the rock, calling out like she's still mid-argument)

Okay, okay — *what about a new bike in SIX months?*

TILLY

(shakes her head firmly, arms crossed but amused)

Nope.

CAMAS

(still peeing, defeated but dramatic)

Ugh. Fine.

(beat)

CAMAS

(softer, genuine)

Love you, sista.

TILLY

(calls back)

Love you, friend.

(Camas stands up, tries to zip her now-unzippable pack. She gives up, laughing. They walk toward the trail.)

(TILLY runs off.)

CAMAS

(chasing after her, yells good naturedly.)

Slow your skinny butt down!

PEDRO

(paws to pick up the handlebars, to audience, softly)

It starts with a friend's pact.

(Optional Chorus Flourish: The Keepers, still holding their cherished objects, slowly step to form a line across the back of the stage, creating a quiet, intentional final tableau of stability and care.)

TILLY

(from offstage, calls)

P, come!

PEDRO

(barks toward Tilly)

(lifts the handlebars for the vow, holding them vertically, high, like a beacon)

The hilltop pact is simple:

For one more year, we choose not to replace what still works.

We choose to mend, to share, to appreciate the things we already hold dear.

We choose not the convenience of the moment, but the promise of the future.

One year. One pact. One planet.

That's all we've got.

And that's more than enough.

(Optional Chorus Flourish: The Keepers, still holding their cherished objects, slowly step to form a line across the back of the stage, creating a quiet, intentional final tableau of stability and care.)

(Blackout.)

The Stuff That's Stuffing Us

Hey, was what Pedro and Tilly said in *The Hilltop Pact* 10-minute play actually true? Let's find out...

"The average U.S. household owns over 300,000 items."

TRUE — A *Los Angeles Times* report, quoting a professional organizer, found that the typical American home contains **more than 300,000 items**. That's a lot of stuff hiding in our closets, drawers, and glove compartments.

"We throw away 81 pounds of clothing per person each year."

TRUE — According to the U.S. EPA, the average American tosses **about 81 pounds of textiles** annually. That's roughly one giant suitcase... every year.

"...Buy a million plastic bottles a minute."

TRUE (globally) — Worldwide, we purchase 1 million plastic bottles every single minute, according to reporting from *National Geographic*. That's a river of bottles that never stops flowing.

"...Lease phones with plans to replace them before we even

love them."

TRUE-ISH — Most phone owners now upgrade every 2–3 years, often because of carrier promotions or lease-style plans. We barely learn our phone's quirks before we send it back into the upgrade carousel.

"If stuff were dogs…"

Pedro metaphor magic — Delightful, but no official statistic compares household clutter to canines (yet).

"Every single day, 13 million phones get tossed."

VERIFIED — The documentary *Buy Now: The Shopping Conspiracy* cites this as a global e-waste scale shocker. Whether recycled, resold, or trashed, millions of phones *do* move through the waste stream daily.

"The production of all that stuff generates 45% of all greenhouse gas emissions."

TRUE — The UN's International Resource Panel reports that the production and consumption of goods—everything from clothing to cars—creates nearly half of global emissions.

"The average piece of clothing is only worn seven times before it's thrown out."

TRUE — A UK study by Barnardo's found that some fast-fashion items are worn just seven times before being discarded. Seven! That's barely a week of wear.

"We're using natural resources 1.7 times faster than the Earth can regenerate them."

TRUE — The Global Footprint Network calculates that humanity is currently living as though we have 1.7 Earths. (Spoiler: we only have one.)

"The average hiker brings 293 of them on day trips."

More Pedro Math — Not a real statistic. But if you've ever cleaned out your backpack, it might *feel* true.

One More Year Pact

I WILL KEEP OR USE ________________________________

FOR ONE MORE YEAR

INSTEAD OF REPLACING IT OUT OF HABIT, BOREDOM, OR CONVENIENCE.

I'M MAKING THIS PERSONAL PROMISE BECAUSE...

CHECK ALL THAT APPLY)

☐ MY BACKPACK IS AUDITIONING FOR HOARDERS: TRAIL EDITION.

☐ I DO NOT, IN FACT, NEED SIX WATER BOTTLES WITH DIFFERENT MOODS.

☐ I WANT TO KEEP MY BIKE AND MY SANITY ONE MORE YEAR.

☐ PEDRO'S FACT CHECKS HIT TOO CLOSE TO HOME.

☐ MY CLOSET SIGHED AT ME. LIKE... AUDIBLY.

☐ I DISCOVERED DUPLICATES OF THINGS I DON'T EVEN REMEMBER BUYING.

☐ I AM NOT A MINIMALIST... BUT EVEN I HAVE LIMITS.

☐ THE PLANET COULD USE A BREATHER, AND SO COULD I.

☐ I'D LIKE TO SPEND MORE TIME OUTSIDE AND LESS TIME SHOPPING ONLINE.

☐ I'M READY TO TRY A TINY REBELLION AGAINST OVERCONSUMPTION.

☐ ____

(MY PERSONAL REASON)

MY COMMITMENT:

I PROMISE TO PAUSE BEFORE PURCHASING.

I PROMISE TO HONOR WHAT I ALREADY HAVE.

I PROMISE TO LET THIS ONE SMALL ACT JOIN A LARGER WAVE OF CARE.

SIGNED,

____

Performance Notes

BLOCKING IDEAS, TECH CUES, REMINDERS

* 9 7 8 1 9 5 3 9 6 5 1 1 0 *